JACQUELINE MITTON holds an MA in Physics from the University of Oxford
and a Doctorate in Astro... from the University of Cambridge. A prolific author of books
and articles on astronom... Oxford Book of Astronomy
(with husband Simon Mitton); ...se Dictionary of Astronomy (OUP);
The Oxford Children's Encyclo... ... Children's Guide to Astronomy,
which was sho... Book Prize 1999.
In 1990, Asteroid 4... ...er husband, Simon.

CHRISTINA BA... ...Royal College of Art.
She has illustrated many boo... ...he Beast by Michael Morpurgo
which was shortlisted for th... ...nmuz by Christopher Moore,
which was commended fo... ...e Labours of Hercules written
by James Riordan and ... *Atlantis*, the first book
she both w... ...great acclaim.

NORTHERN SKY

This star map has the North Celestial Pole at its centre. It shows constellations of the northern sky. Constellations lying across the celestial equator appear on both maps. Paler areas represent the Milky Way.

Constellations of the northern sky featured in this book:

Ursa Major ∽ the Great Bear
Ursa Minor ∽ the Little Bear
Cygnus ∽ the Swan
Vulpecula ∽ the Fox
Leo ∽ the Lion
Taurus ∽ the Bull
Gemini ∽ the Twins
Draco ∽ the Dragon

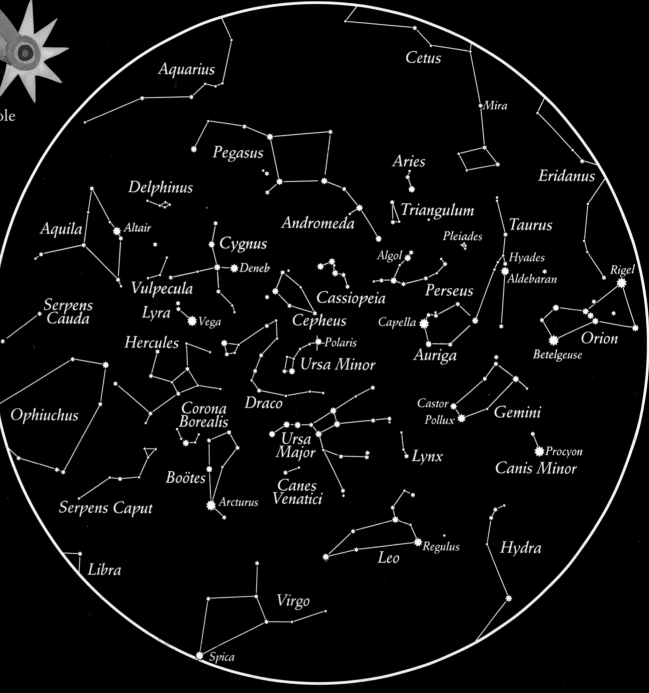

Aquarius
Cetus
Mira
Pegasus
Aries
Eridanus
Delphinus
Triangulum
Taurus
Andromeda
Pleiades
Aquila
Altair
Cygnus
Algol
Hyades
Aldebaran
Deneb
Perseus
Rigel
Vulpecula
Serpens Cauda
Cassiopeia
Lyra
Vega
Cepheus
Capella
Orion
Hercules
Polaris
Betelgeuse
Ursa Minor
Auriga
Draco
Castor
Ophiuchus
Corona Borealis
Pollux
Gemini
Ursa Major
Lynx
Boötes
Canes Venatici
Procyon
Serpens Caput
Canis Minor
Arcturus
Regulus
Libra
Leo
Hydra
Virgo
Spica

+ marks the Celestial Pole

SOUTHERN SKY

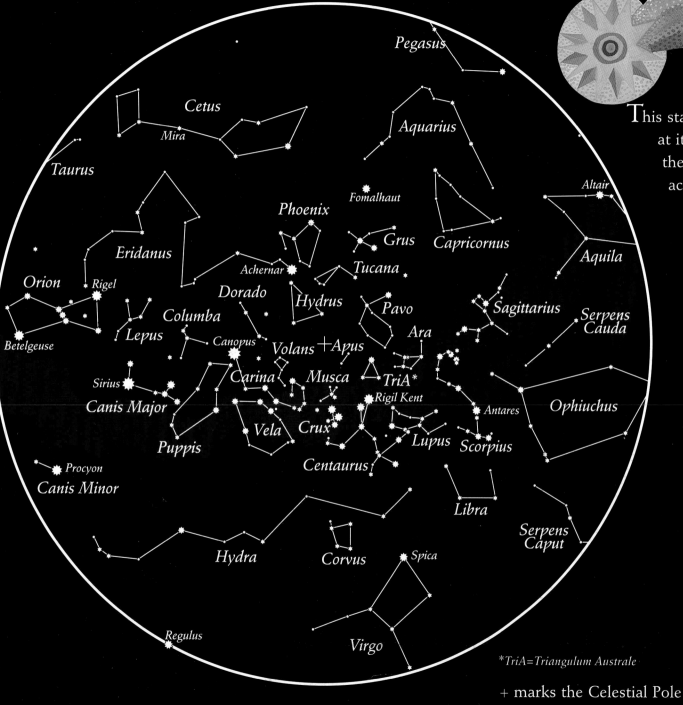

Cetus
Mira
Taurus
Orion
Rigel
Betelgeuse
Eridanus
Columba
Lepus
Sirius
Canis Major
Puppis
Procyon
Canis Minor
Canopus
Carina
Vela
Crux
Hydra
Corvus
Regulus
Virgo
Spica
Centaurus
Musca
Volans +Apus
Dorado
Hydrus
Achernar
Phoenix
Fomalhaut
Grus
Tucana
Pavo
Ara
TriA*
Rigil Kent
Lupus
Scorpius
Antares
Libra
Serpens
Caput
Sagittarius
Ophiuchus
Serpens
Cauda
Aquila
Altair
Capricornus
Aquarius
Pegasus

*TriA=Triangulum Australe

+ marks the Celestial Pole

This star map has the South Celestial Pole at its centre. It shows constellations of the southern sky. Constellations lying across the celestial equator appear on both maps. Paler areas represent the Milky Way.

Constellations of the southern sky featured in this book:

Scorpius ∾ the Scorpion

Lupus ∾ the Wolf

Canis Major ∾ the Great Dog

Lepus ∾ the Hare

Dorado ∾ the Goldfish

Volans ∾ the Flying Fish

Cetus ∾ the Whale

Pavo ∾ the Peacock

Apus ∾ the Bird of Paradise

Tucana ∾ the Toucan

Grus ∾ the Crane

TO MY MOTHER, WHO TAUGHT ME TO LOVE BOOKS AND THE STARS ✦ J.M.

FOR MY GUARDIAN ANGEL, SARAH SLACK ✦ C.B.

First published in Great Britain in 1998 by Frances Lincoln Limited,
4 Torriano Mews, Torriano Avenue, London NW5 2RZ

First paperback edition 1999

British Library Cataloguing in Publication Data
available on request

ISBN 0-7112-1186-8 hardback
ISBN 0-7112-1319-4 paperback

Set in Stone Serif and Trajan

Printed in Hong Kong

9 8 7 6 5 4 3

Zoo in the Sky

A Book of Animal Constellations

Jacqueline Mitton

illustrated by Christina Balit

FRANCES LINCOLN

WHEN THE SUN

sets, darkness falls. The stars appear one by one. Then the sky turns to a picture puzzle. What is hiding in the patterns of stars? Some people say they only see squares and squiggles, lines and loops. But imagine hard, and the sky comes to life. The star patterns make a wing here, a tail there, a twinkling eye, even a scorpion's sting. Sky-watchers long, long ago imagined a whole zoo of animals. They shine there still when you are under the magic spell of the night-time sky.

THE GREAT BEAR

quietly pads her way around the North Pole of the sky. Every day she makes the trip. Two bright stars across her back point straight to the Pole Star. Hanging off the Pole Star by his tail, the Little Bear swings around behind her. You won't see bears quite the same anywhere else – real live bears don't have long tails!

COUNTLESS STARS

light the Milky Way. Along this silvery path, wings outstretched, flies the Swan. On July and August nights, he soars from East to West across the sky. It takes him from dusk till dawn. His eye gleams with a twin star, yellow and blue, called Albireo. He needs a good eye to keep a sharp look-out. The cunning Fox runs beneath him, looking for his dinner.

THE SCORPION has
a nasty sting in his tail. Beware
as he scuttles across the Milky
Way. His tail is curved round
and he is waving his fearsome
claws. Antares, a blood-red
star, glows at his heart. But
the Wolf nearby is not afraid.
After all, he is not such a
friendly creature himself.

LEO THE LION is king of beasts and lord of the sky. In February and March he looks down from a throne high up in the heavens. Stars in his mane shine like jewels in a crown. His brightest star lies close to his heart. That star's name is Regulus, which means 'the little king'.

CHARGING through the zodiac, here comes the Bull. Head down, horns thrust forward, Taurus is ready to toss the Twins. But they are safe, always the other side of the Milky Way. The Bull glowers with a brilliant red eye, the star Aldebaran. A whole cluster of stars is scattered around his nose. The Pleiades huddle behind his shoulder. These starry sisters are not afraid. They know he never looks back.

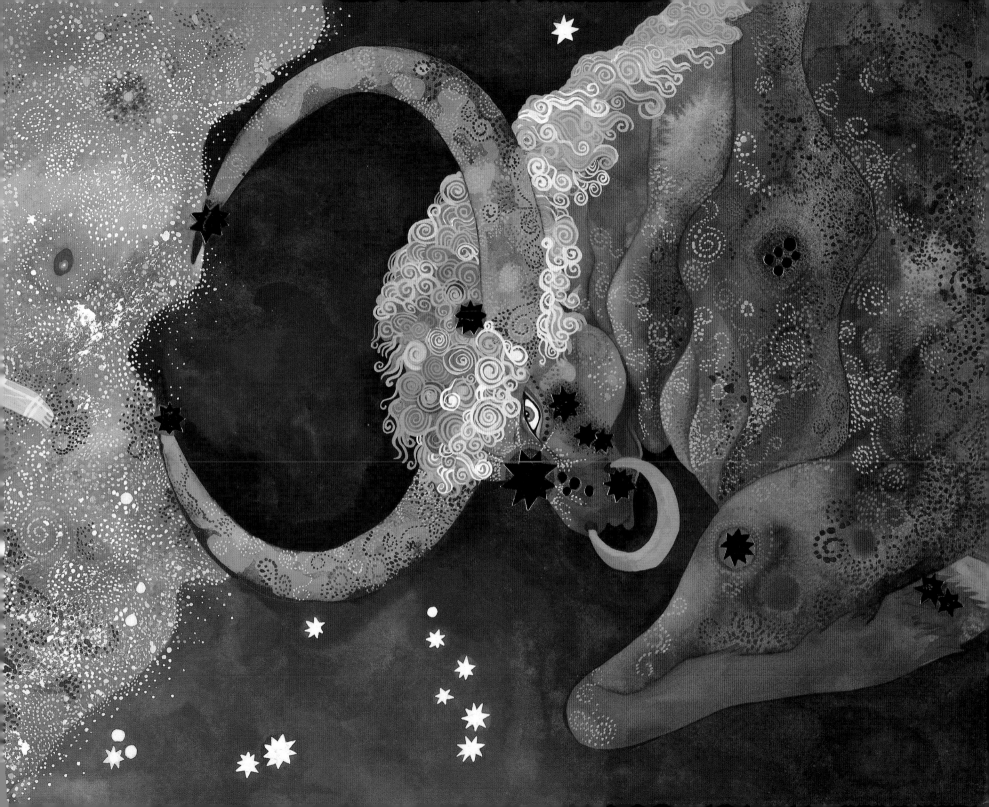

THE GREAT DOG is chasing the Hare, but knows he never can catch it. This dog is a splendid, star-studded creature. His brightest star, Sirius, outshines all others in the night sky. Sirius means 'scorching one' – a good name for a white-hot star. But spot it low in the sky, and Sirius flashes all the colours of the rainbow, like a diamond glinting in sunlight.

DEEP in the southern sky, the glittering Goldfish swims alongside where the good ship Argo sails an ocean of stars. The Flying Fish gives chase in fun, soaring out of the waves. "Now, take care," he warns. "We must not get caught!" But the fish are safe in their starry sea. They will never be anyone's dinner.

THE WHALE is the greatest of all living creatures. He is one of the largest in the sky, too. A monstrous size, he is sometimes called the Sea Monster. On the Whale's back you find Mira, the marvellous star. See how red it glows by his fin. Mira keeps dimming till it disappears; then little by little it brightens once more. About a year later it's back, bright as ever, only to fade all over again.

A ZOO without birds would never do. In the sky there's a whole flock, parading by the South Pole. Tails on display, the Peacock and the Bird of Paradise show off to anyone who watches. The Toucan's glory is his beak, studded with an orange star. The Crane peers at them all, stretching his long neck. Red and blue stars shine on his back.

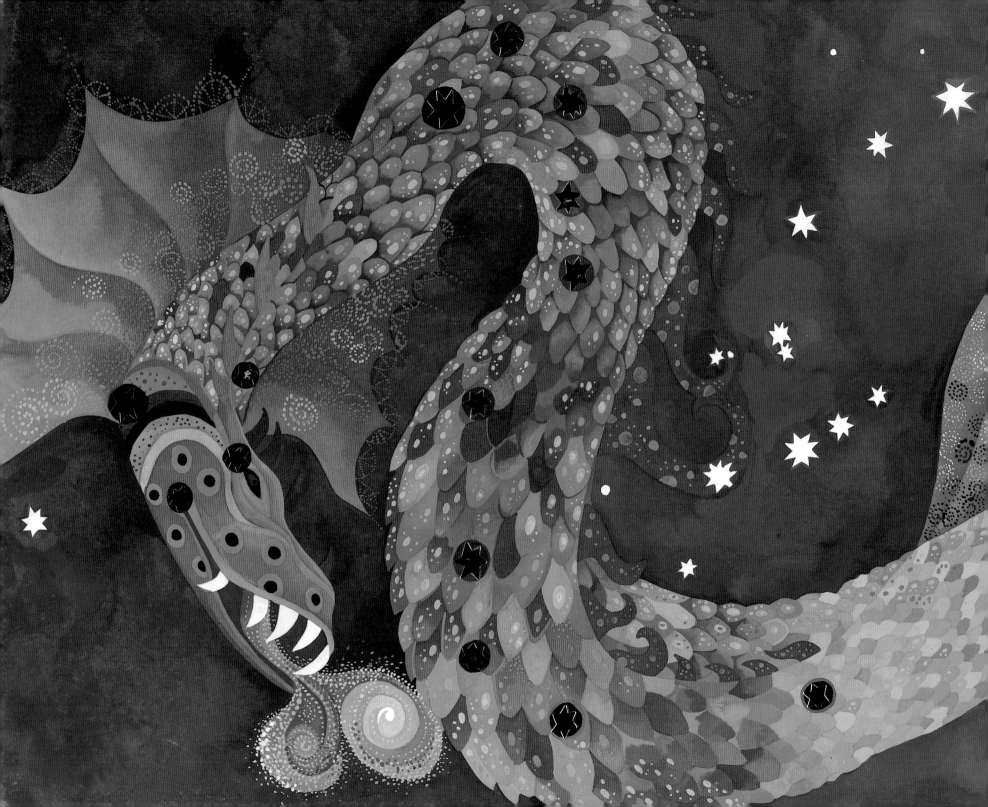

THE LONG, scaly body of the crimson-eyed Dragon coils around the North Pole of the heavens. Take care – he might breathe fire! You won't find a dragon like him in an ordinary zoo. But the starry sky is magic, and one fine sparkly night – who knows – you just might fall under its spell.

What are the stars?

Stars are giant balls of hot gas. They shine because they are so hot. The heat of a star comes from its centre, which creates energy like a natural nuclear power station. Our Sun is a star. It is the only star in our Solar System. The stars of the night sky look much fainter than the Sun, because they are at least 27,000 times further from the Earth.

The sky above you

The Sun rises and sets daily because our Earth spins round once every 24 hours. Like the Sun, some stars rise in the East and set in the West. Each night, these stars rise about 4 minutes earlier than on the night before. This means that the constellations in the night sky gradually change, week by week, month by month. The constellations visible in summer cannot be seen in winter.

The stars in your sky also depend on where you are in the world. Unless you are on the equator, some stars are always hidden below the horizon.

If you are in Europe or North America, for example, you will never see the Peacock or the Southern Cross. If you are in Australia, you will never see the Great Bear or the Little Bear. Some stars, however, circle around the North or South Pole, and never set. They are visible all year round on clear nights, by people far enough North or South to see them.

When you look at Earth maps, East is on the right and West on the left, but on sky maps it is the opposite. The pictures in this book follow sky maps. For example, the Swan, which seems to fly from East to West in the sky, flies left to right across the page.

The Sun, and all the stars you can see without a telescope, belong to a family of thousands of millions of stars that we call our Galaxy. On a clear, dark night, you can see the light from countless stars in our Galaxy concentrated in a misty band across the sky called the Milky Way. Beyond our own Galaxy, there are billions of other galaxies scattered through space.

The constellations

For as far back in time as records go, and probably long before then, people have imagined pictures in the star patterns and given them names. Today, astronomers divide the whole of the sky into 88 constellations, with official Latin names. Every star, however faint, is now included in one constellation or another.

Forty-eight of the constellations are very ancient. They were listed by the Greek astronomer Ptolemy in the second century A.D., but were used even earlier. Most of the others were added by people making star maps between 200 and 400 years ago.

Every year the Sun slowly moves in a circle around the sky, passing through the twelve constellations known as the zodiac: Aries, Taurus, Gemini, Cancer, Leo, Virgo, Libra, Scorpius, Sagittarius, Capricornus, Aquarius and Pisces.

Some star patterns have their own popular names, although they are not whole constellations. The best known is the Plough or Big Dipper, which is made up of seven stars in the Great Bear.

Nearly all the brighter stars in the night sky have individual names. Many of these names were given to them by the ancient Arab astronomers, and have a meaning in their language. For example, Aldebaran means 'the follower'.

NORTHERN SKY

This star map has the North Celestial Pole at its centre. It shows constellations of the northern sky. Constellations lying across the celestial equator appear on both maps. Paler areas represent the Milky Way.

Constellations of the northern sky featured in this book:

Ursa Major ∾ the Great Bear

Ursa Minor ∾ the Little Bear

Cygnus ∾ the Swan

Vulpecula ∾ the Fox

Leo ∾ the Lion

Taurus ∾ the Bull

Gemini ∾ the Twins

Draco ∾ the Dragon

+ marks the Celestial Pole

Aquarius

Cetus

Mira

Pegasus

Aries

Eridanus

Delphinus

Triangulum

Taurus

Aquila

Altair

Andromeda

Pleiades

Cygnus

Algol

Deneb

Hyades

Aldebaran

Vulpecula

Cassiopeia

Perseus

Rigel

Serpens Cauda

Lyra

Cepheus

Capella

Vega

Hercules

Polaris

Auriga

Orion

Betelgeuse

Ursa Minor

Draco

Castor

Ophiuchus

Corona Borealis

Pollux

Gemini

Ursa Major

Lynx

Procyon

Boötes

Canes Venatici

Canis Minor

Serpens Caput

Arcturus

Libra

Regulus

Leo

Hydra

Virgo

Spica

SOUTHERN SKY

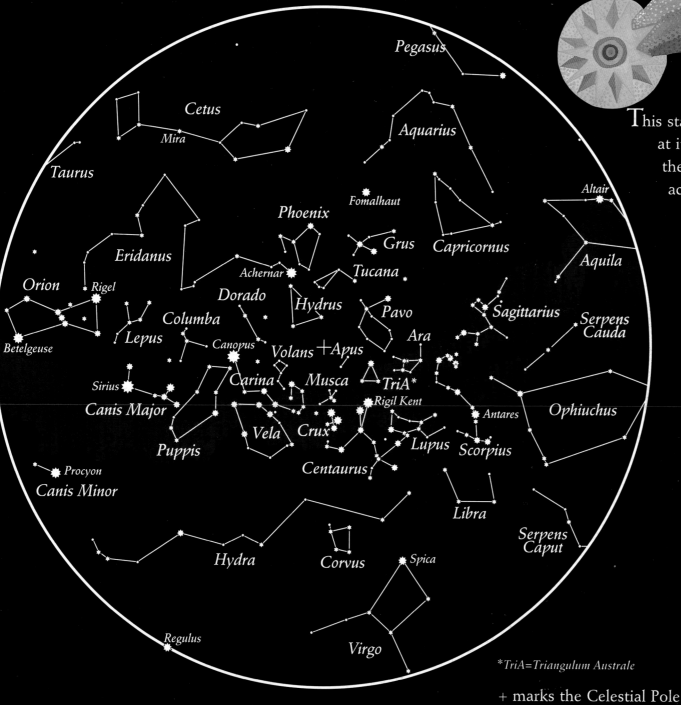

Pegasus

Cetus

Mira

Taurus

Aquarius

Fomalhaut

Phoenix

Grus

Capricornus

Altair

Orion

Rigel

Eridanus

Achernar

Tucana

Aquila

Betelgeuse

Dorado

Hydrus

Pavo

Sagittarius

Serpens Cauda

Columba

Ara

Lepus

Canopus

Volans +Apus

Sirius

Carina

Musca

TriA *

Ophiuchus

Canis Major

Rigil Kent

Antares

Puppis

Vela

Crux

Lupus

Scorpius

Centaurus

Libra

Procyon

Canis Minor

Serpens Caput

Hydra

Corvus

Spica

Regulus

Virgo

*TriA=Triangulum Australe

+ marks the Celestial Pole

This star map has the South Celestial Pole at its centre. It shows constellations of the southern sky. Constellations lying across the celestial equator appear on both maps. Paler areas represent the Milky Way.

Constellations of the southern sky featured in this book:

Scorpius ∽ the Scorpion

Lupus ∽ the Wolf

Canis Major ∽ the Great Dog

Lepus ∽ the Hare

Dorado ∽ the Goldfish

Volans ∽ the Flying Fish

Cetus ∽ the Whale

Pavo ∽ the Peacock

Apus ∽ the Bird of Paradise

Tucana ∽ the Toucan

Grus ∽ the Crane

MORE BOOKS FROM FRANCES LINCOLN
ILLUSTRATED BY CHRISTINA BALIT

ISHTAR AND TAMMUZ

Christopher Moore

Illustrated by Christina Balit

Ishtar, all-powerful queen of the stars, sends her son Tammuz to live on the earth –
and wherever he walks, birds and animals follow him and the earth brings forth fruit
and crops. But when she sees how much he is loved, jealousy hardens his mother's heart...

Suitable for National Curriculum English – Reading, Key Stage 2; History, Key Stage 2
Scottish Guidelines English Language – Reading, Levels C and D; Environmental Studies, Levels C and D

ISBN 0-7112-1099-3   £4.99

BLODIN THE BEAST

Michael Morpurgo

Christopher Moore

Illustrated by Christina Balit

Blodin the beast stalks the land, breathing fire and razing villages to ruins. Only wise old
Shanga, weaving his magic carpet, knows how to destroy the monster, but he is too old
to cross the mountains that never end... A timeless story of a young boy's quest
to save his people, that will entrance children of every age.

Suitable for National Curriculum English – Reading, Key Stage 2
Scottish Guidelines English Language – Reading, Level C

ISBN 0-7112-0910-3   £5.99

ATLANTIS
LEGEND OF A LOST CITY

Christina Balit

When Poseidon marries a beautiful mortal called Cleito, he transforms her island into a rich,
fertile place where he builds a perfect city and names it Atlantis. But as the years pass,
his descendants start to act less like gods and more like men... Based on
Plato's *Timaeus* and *Critias*, with a note by Geoffrey Ashe, this retelling
echoes one of the most haunting themes of humankind.

Suitable for National Curriculum English – Reading, Key Stage 2; History, Key Stage 2
Scottish Guidelines English Language – Reading, Level C; Environmental Studies, Levels B and C

ISBN 0-7112-1417-4   £5.99

Frances Lincoln titles are avaliable from all good bookshops.
Prices are correct at time of publication, but may be subject to change.